W9-BBM-397

An Early I CAN READ Book

LITTLE CHICK'S
STORY

by Mary DeBall Kwitz

Pictures by Cyndy Szekeres

Harper & Row, Publishers

New York, Hagerstown, San Francisco, London

Little Chick's Story
Text copyright © 1978 by Mary DeBall Kwitz
Illustrations copyright © 1978 by Cyndy Szekeres

FIRST EDITION

Library of Congress Cataloging in Publication Data
Kwitz, Mary DeBall.
    Little Chick's story.

    (An Early I can read book)
    SUMMARY: Broody Hen tells Little Chick how she will grow up and have chicks of her own some day.
    [1. Chickens—Fiction]   I. Szekeres, Cyndy.
II. Title.
PZ7.K976Li   [E]   77-11841
ISBN 0-06-023664-7
ISBN 0-06-023666-3 lib. bdg.

For my parents

Mary and Clark DeBall

Broody Hen laid five eggs.

She laid one egg in the hen house
for the farmer's son.

She laid one egg in the barn
for the farmer's daughter.

7

She laid one egg in the meadow

for the ring-tailed raccoon.

And she hid one egg

in the violets

for the Easter rabbit.

"One, two, three, four,"

counted Broody Hen.

Then she laid one more egg.

"This one is for me," she said.

And she fluffed out her feathers

and sat down on her egg.

She sat on it all day

in the sun.

She sat on it all night

in the dark.

She sat on her egg

when the wind blew

and when it rained.

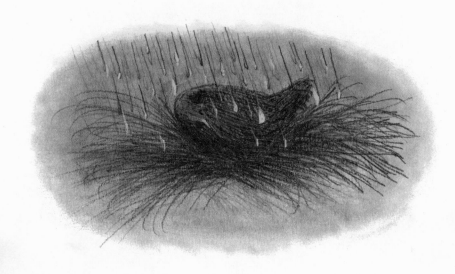

And she clucked

a little hatching-out song.

"My chick-a-dee, my chick-a-dee,

my golden, downy chick-a-dee,

the sun is warm,

the wind blows free,

hatch out for me, my chick-a-dee."

15

And then one sunny, windy day

her egg hatched open.

And out came Little Chick.

Little Chick looked around her.

She looked up at Broody Hen.

"I'm hungry," said Little Chick.

"Eat, my chick-a-dee,"

said Broody Hen,

as she scratched up chicken feed.

Little Chick ran behind her,

pecking and eating,

until her stomach was full.

In the evening Little Chick

crept under Broody Hen's wing.

She peeked out at the dark

and the stars,

and said,

"Tell me a story, Broody Hen."

And Broody Hen did.

"Once upon a time," she said,
"there was a golden, downy
Little Chick.
She ate lots of chicken feed
and ran about in the sun
and the wind.

And she grew strong
and big

until she was a strong,

big Broody Hen.

Then she laid five eggs.

She laid one egg in the hen house

for the farmer's son.

She laid one egg in the barn
for the farmer's daughter.

She laid one egg in the meadow

for the ring-tailed raccoon.

And she hid one egg

in the violets

for the Easter rabbit.

27

Then that Little Chick,

grown strong and big

as a Broody Hen,

counted *One, two, three, four.*

And then she laid

one more egg...."

"Just for herself?"

asked Little Chick.

29

"Yes," said Broody Hen,

"just for herself."

Then Little Chick snuggled up

close to her mother.

And in the dark night,

under the stars,

Little Chick went to sleep.